AMELIA BEDELIA
UNDER
CONSTRUCTION

BY HERMAN PARISH

PICTURES BY LYNN SWEAT

Greenwillow Books, *An Imprint of* HarperCollins*Publishers*

Library of Congress Cataloging-in-Publication Data

Parish, Herman.

Amelia Bedelia under construction / by Herman Parish ; pictures by Lynn Sweat.

p. cm.

"Greenwillow Books."

Summary: When Amelia Bedelia babysits for the Hardy family,

she becomes involved in some unexpected remodeling of their house.

ISBN-10: 0-06-084344-6 (trade bdg.) ISBN-13: 978-0-06-084344-1 (trade bdg.)

ISBN-10: 0-06-084345-4 (lib. bdg.) ISBN-13: 978-0-06-084345-8 (lib. bdg.)

[1. Building—Fiction. 2. Babysitters—Fiction. 3. Humorous stories.]

I. Sweat, Lynn, ill. II. Title.

PZ7.P2185Are 2006 [E]—dc22 2005014897

First Edition 10 9 8 7 6 5 4 3 2 1

 Greenwillow Books

For Manny &
Evelyn Piltin,
Mr. & Mrs. Fix-It
—H. P.

To Jen and Amanda
—L. S.

Amelia Bedelia was out of breath.

"Sorry I am late,"

she said.

"All of these houses look alike."

"I know," said Kathy Hardy.

"Sometimes I get mixed up, too."

"You do?" said Amelia Bedelia.

"I sure do," said Mrs. Hardy.

"I wish our house looked different."

"Tell your husband," said Amelia Bedelia.

"I've heard that he is handy with tools."

Mrs. Hardy sighed. "Bob is very handy,

but he travels way too much.

He's coming home today from a business trip.

He had to talk at a board meeting."

"That is awful," said Amelia Bedelia.

"There is nothing worse

than a bored meeting."

"How true," said Mrs. Hardy.

"Thank you for babysitting

while I go to the doctor."

"Are you sick?" said Amelia Bedelia.

"No," said Mrs. Hardy.

"I am expecting."

"Expecting what?" said Amelia Bedelia.

"An addition," said Mrs. Hardy.

"I can help," said Amelia Bedelia.

"I am pretty good at math."

Mrs. Hardy laughed and said,

"You can help when the addition arrives."

"I will do my best," said Amelia Bedelia.

Just then two children burst out of the house.

"It's Amelia Bedelia!" said Angela.

"Hooray!" said Andrew. "She's here!"

"Hi, kids," said Amelia Bedelia.

"We get to spend all day together."

Mrs. Hardy hugged her children

and got into the car.

"I'll be back this afternoon," she said.

"Amelia Bedelia is in charge.

Do whatever she says."

"We will," said Andrew and Angela.

"Well," said Amelia Bedelia.

"What would be fun to do?"

"Let's play house," said Angela.

"All right," said Amelia Bedelia.

"If you are a house,

then your head is the attic

and your feet are the basement."

"I am not a house," said Andrew.

"Let's play trucks in my sandbox,"

he said.

"Let's think," said Amelia Bedelia.

"What can we do together?"

As they talked, a truck pulled into the driveway.

"Excuse me," said the driver.

"Is this Eighty-one Fairview Avenue?"

"No," said Angela.

"This is number eighteen."

"Oh," said the driver.

"I thought I recognized

this house from the plans."

"What are your plans?"

asked Amelia Bedelia.

"And who are you?"

"My name is Bill," said the driver.

"And this here is Eddie."

"Hey there," said Eddie.

"We are in construction."

"In construction?" said Amelia Bedelia.

"You look like you are in a truck."

Bill smiled as they got out of the truck.

"What Eddie means

 is that we build things."

"What things?" said Andrew.

"Houses," said Eddie.

"We redo kitchens and bathrooms."

"That's right," said Bill.

"We also do additions."

"Additions?" said Amelia Bedelia.

"Say, you guys are right on time.

Mrs. Hardy is expecting an addition."

"Wait a minute," said Bill.

"This is the wrong address.

We're looking for

number eighty-one."

"Excuse me,"

said Amelia Bedelia.

"May I see that address?"

Bill handed it to her.

"This says eighty-one," said Amelia Bedelia.

Then she turned the number upside down.

"Or it can say eighteen."

"Hey," said Eddie. "Look at that."

"Huh," said Bill.

"I guess this is the right place."

"Let's get started," said Eddie.

"Hooray," said Andrew.

Bill unrolled a big piece of paper.

"Here are the plans for your addition."

"Wow," said Angela.

"That is our house. There is my room."

"Of course it is," said Bill.

"These are major improvements.

There's a bigger breakfast room,

a family room, a home office . . . "

"Look here," said Eddie.

"There is even a half bath."

"Ha!" said Amelia Bedelia.

"That is pretty dumb, if you ask me.

Water will run out of half a bathtub."

"There is no bathtub," said Eddie.

"Just a toilet and sink."

"That's smarter," said Amelia Bedelia.

"A half bath would leave you half-dirty."

"Speaking of dirt," said Bill,

"let's go out back and figure out

where we will break ground."

"Great!" said Amelia Bedelia.

"I'll be right back."

She ran to the garage.

Bill and Eddie gave extra hard hats

to Angela and Andrew.

Then everyone walked

to the backyard.

"First off," said Bill, "we'll measure

to see where the addition will be."

Eddie held a stake.

Andrew pounded it.

They tied string between the stakes.

Amelia Bedelia returned with three hammers.

"Here you go," said Amelia Bedelia.

"I found these in your dad's toolbox.

Okay, kids. Let's hit it!"

"What are you doing?" said Bill.

"Breaking ground," said Amelia Bedelia.

"Anything else you need broken?"

"I need a coffee break," said Eddie.

"Just don't hammer on my cup."

"We won't," said Amelia Bedelia.

"It's time we had a snack, too."

"Good," said Andrew. "I'm tired.

Being in construction is hard work."

"Come along, you two,"

said Amelia Bedelia.

"Let them do their work,

and we'll do ours."

They went into the kitchen.

Amelia Bedelia made a snack.

"What is our work?" said Angela.

"It is right here," said Amelia Bedelia.

"When I got the hammers

from your dad's workshop,

I found his to-do list."

She read out loud: "Sand the deck."

"I know why," said Andrew.

"Dad says it will keep us from getting splinters."

"This deck is big,"

 said Amelia Bedelia.

"We will need a lot of sand."

"Hey," said Andrew.

"My sandbox is full of sand."

"I'll get some buckets," said Angela.

 In no time, the deck was sanded.

"This is great," said Angela.

"It's like having our own beach."

"Without splinters," said Andrew.

"What's next?" said Amelia Bedelia.

"Paint patio chairs," read Andrew.

"Paint is messy," said Amelia Bedelia.

"Look," said Angela.

"Dad wrote, 'Use two coats.'"

"Coats are easy,"

  said Amelia Bedelia.

"Closets are full of them.

  Come along, kids."

They took every last coat.

"That reminds me," said Angela.

"Mom wants a walk-in closet."

"She got her wish," said Amelia Bedelia.

"Now that these coats are gone,

there is room to walk in."

"Let's try it," said Andrew.

"First things first," said Amelia Bedelia.

"Go and put two coats on each chair.

I'll clean out the rest of the closet."

Amelia Bedelia finished

just as the children returned.

"That's that," said Angela.

"Every chair got two coats."

"Nice work," said Amelia Bedelia.

Andrew checked it off the list.

"Let's walk in the closet," he said.

They squeezed into the closet.

"This is a tight fit," said Amelia Bedelia.

"We can't walk at all," said Angela.

"I can't even breathe," said Andrew.

"Mom will have to walk in by herself.

Let's get out of here."

"Whew!" said Amelia Bedelia.

"What else did your mom want?"

"Well," said Angela,

"Mom always talks about

 redoing the kitchen."

"Okay," said Amelia Bedelia.

"Let's see what we can do."

"You mean redo," said Andrew.

 They headed to the kitchen.

"You know what?" said Angela.

"Mom wants marble countertops."

"That is odd," said Amelia Bedelia.

"Who has that many marbles?"

"I do," said Andrew.

"I'll get them."

Amelia Bedelia made flour paste.

They put a dab on each marble.

Soon every countertop

was a marble countertop.

"I had my doubts about this,"

said Amelia Bedelia,

"but it is much prettier now.

What else does your mom want?"

"A picture window," said Angela.

"All right," said Amelia Bedelia.

"Get some paper and colored pencils."

The children drew and drew.

"Let's draw pictures

for every window," said Andrew.

"Nice idea," said Angela.

"Yes," said Amelia Bedelia.

"Every window deserves a picture.

That way, you get a nice view

no matter what is outside."

BRI-INNNNG went the telephone.

"I'll get it," said Amelia Bedelia.

"You two keep drawing."

"Hello," said Amelia Bedelia.

"Hi, honey," said Mr. Hardy. "I'm back.

I'm taking a cab from the airport."

"Well," said Amelia Bedelia,

"make sure you give it back.

Someone else might need it."

"Who is this?" said Mr. Hardy.

"This is Amelia Bedelia," she said.

"This is Bob Hardy," he said.

"I forgot that you are babysitting."

"We've been busy," said Amelia Bedelia.

"How was your bored meeting?"

"Pretty exciting," said Mr. Hardy.

"I told the company president

how to save a lot of money.

Afterward my boss told me

I had hit the nail on the head,

and that the board got the point."

"Oh, I get it," said Amelia Bedelia.

"You mean real boards.

Bring a bunch of nails home.

You can help with the addition."

"What addition?" said Mr. Hardy.

"You know," said Amelia Bedelia.

"The one your wife is expecting."

"That is a secret," said Mr. Hardy.

"Only our family knows right now."

"Not anymore," said Amelia Bedelia.

"Your addition is being delivered."

"Has labor started?" said Mr. Hardy.

"We haven't even picked out a name!"

"The labor is fast," said Amelia Bedelia.

"And their names are Bill and Eddie."

"We've got twins?" yelled Mr. Hardy.

"I doubt it," said Amelia Bedelia.

"Bill is way taller than Eddie."

"Arrgh!" yelled Mr. Hardy.

"I must be losing my marbles!"

"You're in luck," said Amelia Bedelia.

"Your countertops are covered with them.

We can replace any marbles you lose."

Mr. Hardy hung up.

"Poor guy," said Amelia Bedelia.

"He must be tired from hitting nails

on the head into that board.

At least he was not bored."

"Was that our dad?" said Andrew.

"Yes," said Amelia Bedelia.

"He will be home soon."

"You know," said Angela,

"maybe Dad wouldn't go away

if he had a board at home."

"Yes," said Andrew.

"He could meet with it anytime."

"Let's ask Bill," said Angela.

"He must have lots of boards."

"Good idea," said Amelia Bedelia.

They went to the backyard.

Bill and Eddie were still hard at work.

"You have made a lot of progress,"

  said Amelia Bedelia.

"That's right," said Eddie.

"We've kept our noses to the grindstone."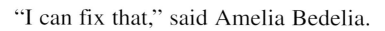

"Ouch!" said Amelia Bedelia.

"Who needs a sharp nose?"

  Bill chuckled and said,

"I hope we don't

  run out of stakes."

"I can fix that," said Amelia Bedelia.

"In the meantime,

  can you help us?

  We need a board."

Eddie found a long board

in the back of their truck.

"Here's a nice one," he said.

"It doesn't have any knots in it."

"I hope not," said Amelia Bedelia.

"We could never untie them."

"It's too long for Dad's desk,"

said Angela. "Can you cut it?"

"Sure," said Bill.

"How long do you want it?"

"A long time," said Amelia Bedelia.

"Mr. Hardy will need it for years."

Bill scratched his head and said,

"I'll cut you a long piece and a short one."

"That's smart," said Amelia Bedelia.

"He can have a long or short board meeting."

Amelia Bedelia and the children went inside.

"Hmmm," said Amelia Bedelia.

"I wonder how many steaks Bill needs?

I'd better thaw some chicken, too."

"Here comes Mom," said Andrew.

Mrs. Hardy pulled into the driveway.

"Oh, good," said Amelia Bedelia.

"Mrs. Hardy will be so pleased

that her addition has arrived.

Let's go and tell her."

Mrs. Hardy got out of her car.

"Whose truck is this?" she said.

"It belongs to Bill and Eddie,"
  said Amelia Bedelia.

"Who are they?" said Mrs. Hardy.

"They are delivering your addition,"
  said Amelia Bedelia.

"Isn't that what you were expecting?"
  Bill and Eddie came around to the front.

"We're finished for the day," said Bill.

"Finished what?" asked Mrs. Hardy.

"When my husband gets home,
  we'll *all* be finished."

Just then a taxicab pulled up.

Mr. Hardy jumped out.

"Good grief," he said.

"What is going on here?"

Everybody tried to explain.

Nobody made any sense.

"Don't blame Bill and Eddie,"

said Amelia Bedelia.

"I am the one who thought

the house number was upside down.

Now everything is upside down."

Mr. Hardy headed to the backyard.

"What's happened to our . . . whoa!"

"Be careful," said Amelia Bedelia.

"You fell into your half bath."

"My what?" said Mr. Hardy.

He got up and brushed himself off.

"What have you done to our deck?"

"We sanded it," said Andrew.

"Now you won't have to."

"These chairs," Mr. Hardy said.

"What's going on with these chairs?"

"They've got two coats," said Angela,

"just like you wanted."

Mr. Hardy stepped into the kitchen.

"Who covered our counters with marbles?"

"We did," said Andrew and Angela.

Mr. Hardy was speechless.

"So, Mr. Hardy," said Amelia Bedelia,

"how do you like your addition so far?"

"Addition?" said Mr. Hardy.

"Sand on the deck, coats on chairs,

countertops covered in marbles . . .

You call this an addition?

This is more like a subtraction!"

Bill and Eddie began to back away.

"Hey," said Andrew. "Don't go.

When will we get our addition?"

"In about six months," said his mom.

"Don't you remember?

That is when we said our new baby—

our addition—will arrive."

"Congratulations!" said Amelia Bedelia.

Bill and Eddie chimed in, too.

"Thank you," said Mr. and Mrs. Hardy.

Angela gave her father the boards.

"Here, Daddy,"

said Angela.

"You can have your next

board meeting at home.

You won't have to go away."

Mr. Hardy nodded.

Then he hugged

Andrew and Angela.

"Thank you," said Mr. Hardy.

"I promise to try to stay home more."

"Honey," said Mrs. Hardy.

"I know that this is a mess,

but maybe it was meant to be.

These plans are perfect

for a house just like ours.

We'll need more room soon."

"You're right, Kathy," said Mr. Hardy.

"We will need this addition

once *our* addition arrives."

Bill and Eddie promised to return

after they finished Eighty-one Fairview.

The Hardys had a lot to celebrate.

They invited Bill and Eddie

to stay for a cookout.

"Amelia Bedelia," said Bill,

"your steaks look tastier

than our stakes."

"Thank you," said Amelia Bedelia.

They all sat down to dinner.

"What a big day," said Mrs. Hardy.

"You never know how things

will add up."

"I do," said Amelia Bedelia.

"I am expecting, too."

"What!" said Mrs. Hardy.

"An addition?"

"That's right," said Amelia Bedelia.

"My addition is this lemon meringue pie.

I am expecting everyone to enjoy it."

And that is exactly what they did.